Animal Detectives
Search for the Facts

SNAKES

Anne O'Daly

Published by Brown Bear Books Ltd
4877 N. Circulo Bujia
Tucson, AZ 85718
USA

and

Unit 3/R, Leroy House
436 Essex Rd
London N1 3QP
UK

© 2020 Brown Bear Books Ltd

ISBN 978-1-78121-450-3 (library bound)
ISBN 978-1-78121-560-9 (paperback)

All rights reserved. No part of this book may be reproduced, stored in a retrieval system, or transmitted, in any form or by any means, electronic, mechanical, photocopying, recording, or otherwise, without the prior written permission of the copyright holder.

Library of Congress Cataloging-in-Publication Data available on request

Design Manager: Keith Davis
Children's Publisher: Anne O'Daly
Picture Manager: Sophie Mortimer

Picture Credits
Cover: iStock: Matt Cole; Interior: iStock: Uwe Bergwitz 16, Steve Byland 5r, EcoPic 4l; Shutterstock: Chantelle Bosch 18, Cappa Photo 5br, Rich Carey 4–5c, 12, Ken Griffiths 4bl, 4–5b, 20, Aptyp_Kok 5tr (inset), D. Kucharski K. Kucharski 5tl, Marie Kassia Ott 8, ShutterOK 5tr, Audrey Snider-Bell 14, Achin Subran 6, Yash 10.
t=top, r=right, l=left, c=center, b=bottom
All artwork and other photography Brown Bear Books.

Brown Bear Books has made every attempt to contact the copyright holder.
If you have any information about omissions, please contact: licensing@brownbearbooks.co.uk

Manufactured in the United States of America
CPSIA compliance information: Batch#AG/5634

Websites
The website addresses in this book were valid at the time of going to press. However, it is possible that contents or addresses may change following publication of this book. No responsibility for any such changes can be accepted by the author or the publisher. Readers should be supervised when they access the Internet.

Contents

Meet the Family 4

Animal Files
   Anaconda 6
   Rainbow Boa 8
   King Cobra 10
   Sea Krait 12
   Western Diamondback Rattlesnake ... 14
   Puff Adder 16
   Sidewinder 18
   Taipan 20

Quiz 22

Glossary 23

Find out More 24

Index 24

Meet the Family

Snakes are reptiles. They are hunters. Some snakes kill with venom. Others squeeze their victims to death. Read on to find out more!

Puff Adder

Sea Krait

Taipan

Sidewinder

Snakes

Rainbow Boa

Anaconda

The western diamondback is a rattlesnake. It is the most dangerous snake in North America.

Western Diamondback Rattlesnake

King Cobra

Anaconda

The green anaconda is the world's biggest snake. It wraps its body around an animal. It squeezes til the animal stops breathing.

FACT FILE

Scientific name: *Eunectes murinus*

Food: deer, chickens, dogs, birds, turtles, other reptiles

Habitat: swamps, rivers, lakes

Where in the World: South America

Tail

Anacondas are good swimmers. They live in rivers and lakes.

WHERE DOES IT LIVE?

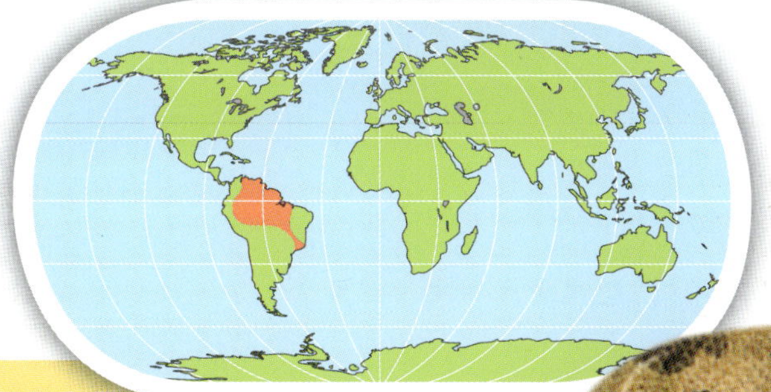

Snakes

Head

Strong body

Scales

BIG OR SMALL

6 feet (1.8 m)

Up to 33 feet (10 m)

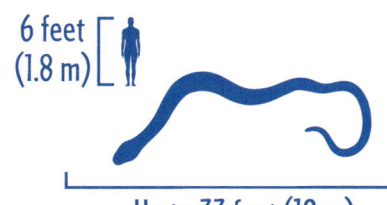

Anacondas open their mouths wide. They swallow prey whole. They can swallow a jaguar!

Rainbow Boa

The rainbow boa is a colorful snake. It is a constrictor. Constrictors kill prey by squeezing it.

FACT FILE

Scientific Name: *Epicrates cenchria*

Food: mammals

Habitat: rain forests, woodlands, grasslands

Where in the World: Central and South America

Smooth, shiny scales

Rainbow boas shine with rainbow colors. That gives the snake its name.

WHERE DOES IT LIVE?

 Snakes

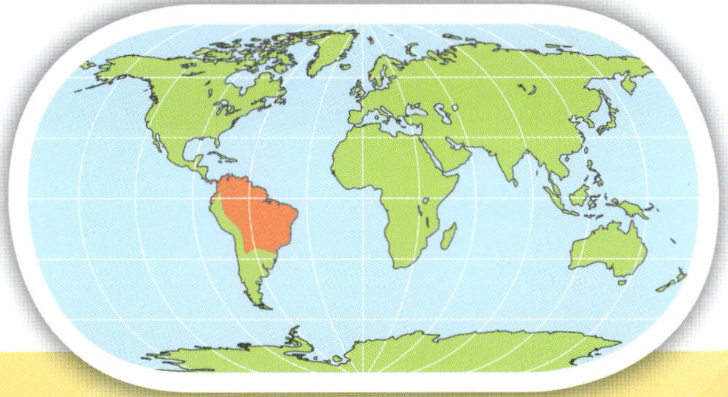

Head

Heat pits sense heat

BIG OR SMALL

6 feet (1.8 m)

Up to 6.5 feet (2 m)

Rainbow boas sense heat from other animals. They can find prey in the dark.

9

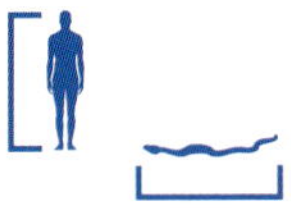

King Cobra

King cobras have deadly venom. One bite can kill an elephant! This snake has a scary hood.

FACT FILE

Scientific Name: *Ophiophagus hannah*

Food: mainly other snakes, sometimes lizards, birds, and eggs

Habitat: forests and swamps, often stay near streams

Where in the World: India and Southeast Asia

Long, thin body

The female makes a nest of leaves. She lays her eggs in it.

WHERE DOES IT LIVE?

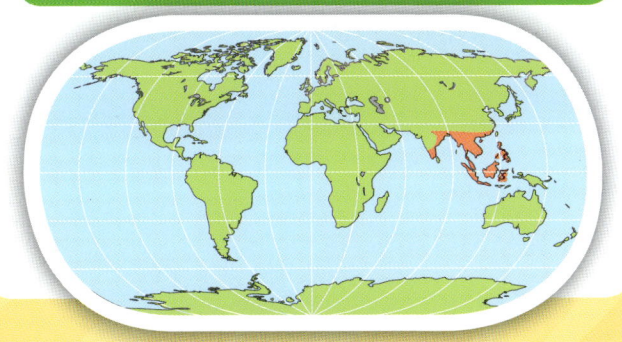

Snakes

Fangs inject venom

Hood of skin

Rears up to attack

King cobras have good senses. They can see from 330 feet (100 m) away. They smell with their tongue. They pick up heat waves.

BIG OR SMALL

6 feet (1.8 m)

up to 18 feet (5.5 m)

11

Sea Krait

Sea kraits live in the sea.
They come on land to lay eggs.
They hunt fish in coral reefs.

FACT FILE

Scientific Name: *Laticauda colubrina*

Food: mainly eels

Habitat: coral reefs

Where in the World: Southeast Asia and northern Australia

White body with black stripes

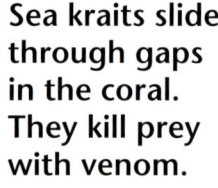

Sea kraits slide through gaps in the coral. They kill prey with venom.

WHERE DOES IT LIVE?

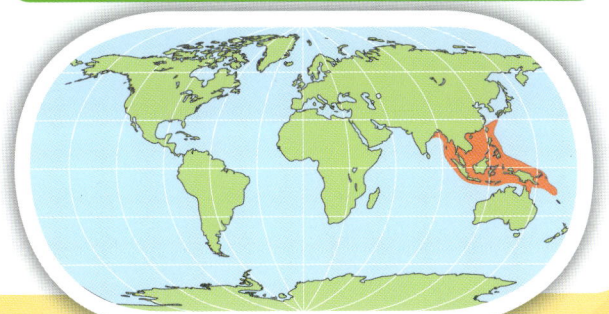

Snakes

Tail shaped like a paddle

Flat body

Nostrils on top of head

Sea kraits can hold their breath for 30 minutes. They can dive to 500 feet (150 m).

BIG OR SMALL

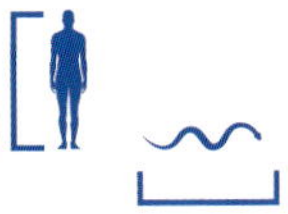

6 feet (1.8 m)

Up to 6.5 feet (2 m)

Western Diamondback Rattlesnake

This snake lives in North America. It has a rattle of loose scales. The rattle warns you to stay away.

FACT FILE

Scientific Name: *Crotalus atrox*

Food: prairie dogs, ground squirrels, gophers, mice, and rats

Habitat: deserts, semideserts, dry grasslands

Where in the World: North America

Rattle shakes from side to side

The snake kills prey with poison. Its long fangs bite the victim.

WHERE DOES IT LIVE?

Snakes

Head

Diamond markings

BIG OR SMALL

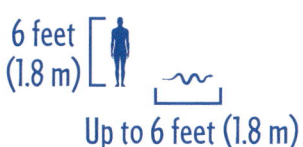

6 feet (1.8 m)

Up to 6 feet (1.8 m)

The snake's rattle is made of keratin. That's the same stuff as your fingernails.

15

Puff Adder

The puff adder is a large snake. It puffs up its body. It does this when it is scared.

FACT FILE

Scientific Name: *Bitis arietans*

Food: birds, toads, lizards, and mammals

Habitat: almost anywhere, apart from thick forests and very dry deserts

Where in the World: Africa

Large head

Puff adders move in a line. Most snakes move from side to side.

WHERE DOES IT LIVE?

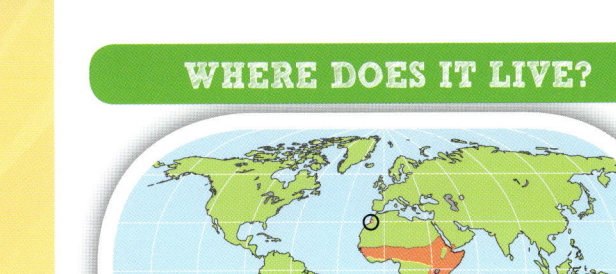

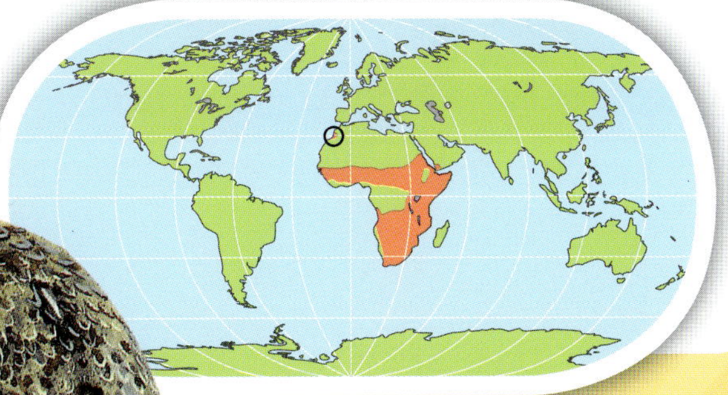

Snakes

V-shaped marks on back

Thick body

BIG OR SMALL

6 feet (1.8 m)

Up to 6 feet (1.8 m)

Puff adders have live babies. The babies grow inside eggs. The eggs hatch in the mom's body.

17

Sidewinder

Sidewinders are rattlesnakes.
They live in hot deserts.
They slide sideways across the sand.

FACT FILE

Scientific Name: *Crotalus cerastes*

Food: lizards, rodents, birds

Habitat: deserts

Where in the World: Southwestern North America

Narrow body

Sidewinders hide in the sand. You can only see their eyes.

WHERE DOES IT LIVE?

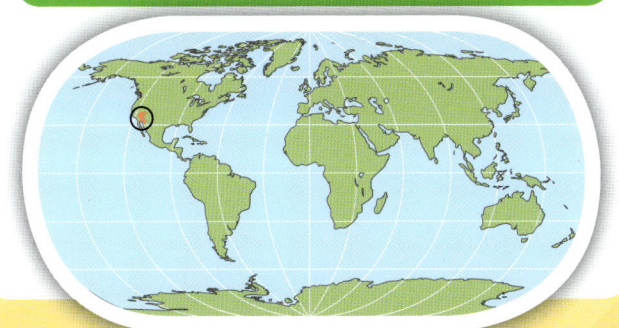

Snakes

Horn-shaped scales

Colors and patterns blend in with the sand

Sidewinders have horns above their eyes. The horns protect the eyes from the sun.

BIG OR SMALL

12 in (30cm)

Up to 30 in (76 cm)

Taipan

There are two types of taipans.
One type lives near the coast.
The other lives inland. Both are deadly!

FACT FILE

Scientific Name: *Oxyuranus*

Food: mammals

Habitat: forests, wooded grassland (coastal taipan); dry flood plains (inland taipan)

Where in the World: Australia

Tube-shaped body

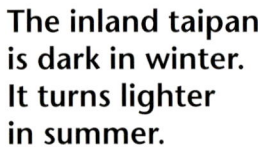

The inland taipan is dark in winter. It turns lighter in summer.

WHERE DOES IT LIVE?

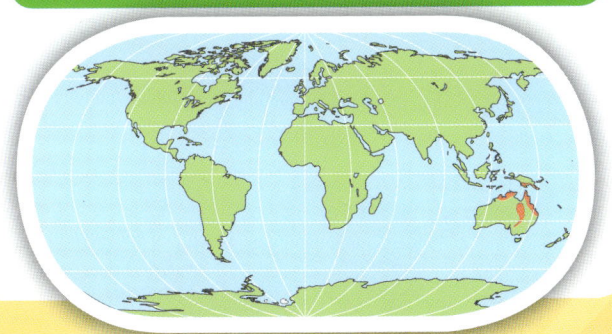

Snakes

Narrow head

The inland taipan has the strongest venom of any snake. One bite could kill 100 people!

Brown scales

BIG OR SMALL

6 feet (1.8 m)
Up to 12 feet (3.6 m)

Coastal taipan

Quiz

Test your skills! Can you answer these questions? Look in the book for clues. The answers are on page 24.

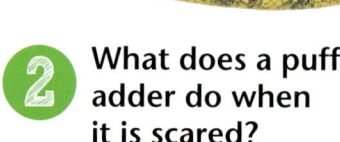

2 What does a puff adder do when it is scared?

1 How does this snake kill its prey?

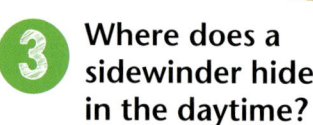

4 Where do sea kraits go to lay their eggs?

3 Where does a sidewinder hide in the daytime?

Glossary

 Snakes

fangs
Long, pointed teeth.

habitat
The kind of place where an animal usually lives.

mammal
An animal that feeds its young on milk. Most mammals have fur or hair.

prey
An animal that is hunted by other animals.

reptile
Animals with a scaly skin.

venom
Poison that some snakes make.

Find out More

Books

Slither, Snake!, Shelby Alinsky (National Geographic Kids, 2015)

Super Snakes (Reptile Adventures), Rebecca Johnson (Windmill Books, 2018)

Websites

animals.sandiegozoo.org/animals/snake

dkfindout.com/uk/animals-and-nature/reptiles/snakes/

www.kidzone.ws/lw/snakes/facts.htm

Index

constrictor 8

eggs 10, 13, 17

fangs 11, 14

mammals 8, 16, 20,

nest 10

prey 7, 8, 9, 12, 14

rattlesnakes 5, 14, 18

reptiles 4, 6,

scales 7, 8, 14, 19, 21

senses 11

venom 4, 10, 11, 12, 21

Quiz Answers: 1. The anaconda squeezes its prey to death. **2.** It puffs up its body. **3.** It hides in the sand with just its eyes showing. **4.** They come onto land to lay their eggs.